OLIVIA
and the
Fairy Princesses

written and illustrated by Ian Falconer

SIMON AND SCHUSTER

LONDON   NEW YORK   SYDNEY   TORONTO   NEW DELHI

With deepest apologies to Martha Graham

SIMON AND SCHUSTER
First published in Great Britain in 2012
by Simon and Schuster UK Ltd
1st Floor, 222 Gray's Inn Road, London, WC1X 8HB
A CBS Company

Originally published in 2012 by Atheneum Books for Young Readers,
an imprint of Simon and Schuster Children's Publishing Division,
New York

Book design by Ann Bobco
The text for this book is set in Centaur.
The illustrations for this book are rendered in
charcoal and gouache on paper.

A CIP catalogue record for this book is available from
the British Library upon request

ISBN: 978 0 85707 887 2 (hardback)
ISBN: 978 0 85707 906 0 (eBook)

Printed in China

10 9 8 7 6 5 4 3 2 1

Olivia was depressed.

"I think I'm having
an identity crisis,"
she told her parents.

"I don't know what I should be!"

"Well," said her father, "you'll always be my little princess!"

"That's the problem," said Olivia. "All the girls want to be princesses."

"At Pippa's birthday party, they were all dressed in big, pink, ruffly skirts with sparkles and little crowns and sparkly wands. Including some of the boys.

I chose a simple French sailor shirt, matador trousers,
black flats, a strand of pearls, sunglasses, a red bag,
and my gardening hat."

"Why is it always a pink princess? Why not an Indian princess or a princess from Thailand or an African princess or a princess from China?

There *are* alternatives."

"For the school dance recital, *everyone* was trying out for the fairy princess ballerina. Even a couple of the boys."

"But, Olivia," said her mother,
"I seem to remember last year
you wanting to be a ballerina."

"That was when I was little."

"I'm trying to develop a more stark, modern style."

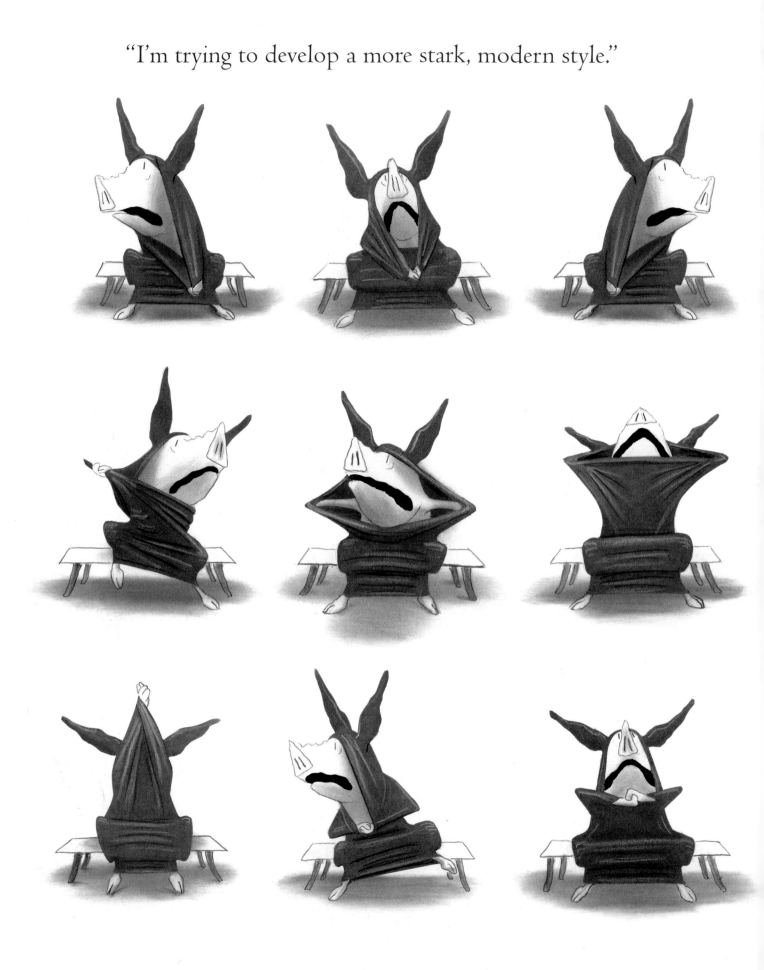

"Olivia, it's time for your bath," said her mother.

"And on Halloween,"
said Olivia, "what did
all the girls go as?"

"I went
as a
warthog.

It was
very
effective."

"If everyone's a princess, then princesses aren't special anymore!" said Olivia.

"Why do they all want to be the same?"

After her bath, Olivia's mother read her a story. It was about a beautiful maiden who was locked in a tower by an evil queen.

"'When a prince came along, rescued her, and made her his—'"

"Not his princess!" cried Olivia.

"Fine," said her mother, who was tiring of this discussion. "I'll read you the story of the Little Match Girl. 'Once there was a little girl who was forced to sell matches barefoot in the snow.

The matches kept her warm for a while, but all too soon they ran out. . .'"

"Oh, Mummy, that's so sad," said Olivia, tearing up.
"I may not want to be a princess, but I wouldn't
want to be freezing in the snow."

Her mother said, "Well, I want you to be ASLEEP
in five minutes!"

"But first read me the story about Little Red Riding Hood!"

"No, Olivia, it's bedtime."

"Just the parts
where everyone
gets eaten.
Please?"

"No. I'm
turning out
the light."

Olivia lay in the dark trying to sleep,
but her brain wouldn't let her.

"Maybe I could be a nurse and devote myself
to the sick and the elderly.

"I could use my brothers to practise bandaging.

And various other treatments."

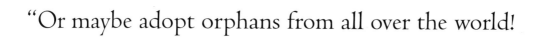

"Or maybe adopt orphans from all over the world!

Or I could be a reporter and
expose corporate malfeasance."

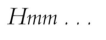

Hmm . . .

Then it occurred to her.
"I know. . ."

"I want to be queen."